Dear Parent:

Congratulations! Your child is taking the first steps on an exciting journey. The destination? Independent reading!

STEP INTO READING® will help your child get there. The program offers five steps to reading success. Each step includes fun stories and colorful art. There are also Step into Reading Sticker Books, Step into Reading Math Readers, Step into Reading Phonics Readers, Step into Reading Write-In Readers, and Step into Reading Phonics Boxed Sets—a complete literacy program with something to interest every child.

Learning to Read, Step by Step!

Ready to Read Preschool–Kindergarten
• big type and easy words • rhyme and rhythm • picture clues
For children who know the alphabet and are eager to begin reading.

Reading with Help Preschool–Grade 1
• basic vocabulary • short sentences • simple stories
For children who recognize familiar words and sound out new words with help.

Reading on Your Own Grades 1–3
• engaging characters • easy-to-follow plots • popular topics
For children who are ready to read on their own.

Reading Paragraphs Grades 2–3
• challenging vocabulary • short paragraphs • exciting stories
For newly independent readers who read simple sentences with confidence.

Ready for Chapters Grades 2–4
• chapters • longer paragraphs • full-color art
For children who want to take the plunge into chapter books but still like colorful pictures.

STEP INTO READING® is designed to give every child a successful reading experience. The grade levels are only guides. Children can progress through the steps at their own speed, developing confidence in their reading, no matter what their grade.

Remember, a lifetime love of reading starts with a single step!

For Buddy —D.F.

Step into Reading, Random House, and the Random House colophon are registered trademarks of Random House, Inc.

Visit us on the Web!
StepIntoReading.com
randomhouse.com/kids

Educators and librarians, for a variety of teaching tools, visit us at
RHTeachersLibrarians.com

ISBN: 978-0-7364-3026-5 (trade) — ISBN: 978-0-7364-8121-2 (lib. bdg.)

Printed in the United States of America   10 9 8 7 6 5 4 3 2 1

Disney
Lady and the TRAMP

Adapted by Delphine Finnegan

Illustrated by the Disney Storybook Artists

Random House 🏠 New York

One Christmas morning,
Jim Dear gave Darling
a surprise.
She opened the gift box.
A pretty new puppy
popped out.
Jim Dear and Darling
called her Lady.

Lady watched
over the house.
She took care
of everyone—
even the fish.

Lady had good friends.
She had a great life.

Then Jim Dear
and Darling
had a baby.

Lady was happy.
She would take care
of the baby, too.

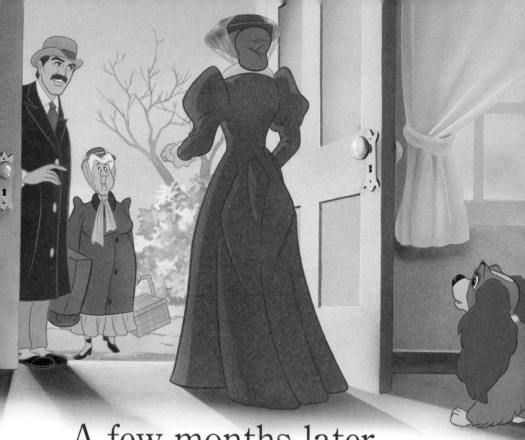

A few months later,
Jim Dear and Darling
took a trip.
Aunt Sarah came
to watch the baby.
She had many bags.

Two cats popped out
of one bag.
They surprised Lady.

The cats made a mess.

Lady stopped them.

Aunt Sarah thought

Lady had made the mess.

"Bad dog,"
said Aunt Sarah.
She made Lady
wear a muzzle.

Lady ran away.

Mean dogs chased her.

Tramp was a nice dog.

He was a stray.

He did not have a home.

Tramp liked
to help other dogs.

He would help Lady.

Tramp snarled.

He bared his teeth.

The mean dogs ran away.

Tramp saved Lady.

Next,
Tramp led Lady
to the zoo.

At the zoo,

a beaver chewed

through the muzzle.

Lady was free!

Tramp took Lady
to dinner.
They ate spaghetti
and meatballs.

The chefs sang songs.

It was a beautiful night.

Lady and Tramp

fell in love.

When Lady went home,
she had to stay outside.
Aunt Sarah
tied her to a chain.

No one could
cheer Lady up.

That night,

Lady saw a rat.

The rat climbed

into the baby's bedroom.

Lady barked and barked.

Aunt Sarah woke up.

"Be quiet,"

she said.

Tramp heard Lady, too.

He wanted to help.

He ran into the house.

He snarled and snapped
at the rat.

Lady was still scared.

She had to take care

of the baby.

She broke her chain.

Tramp caught the rat.

The baby was safe.

Lady and Tramp
made a great team.

Now it was Lady's turn
to help Tramp.
Jim Dear and Darling
came home that night.

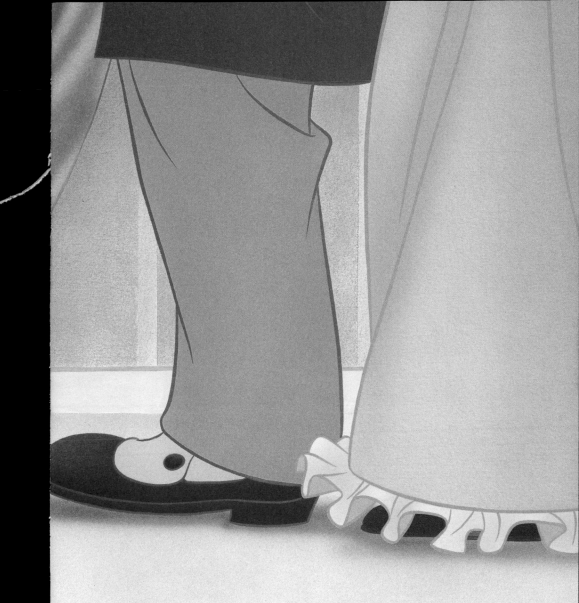

Lady showed them how
Tramp had helped her.
Tramp had a new home!

The next Christmas,
the family grew.
Lady loved taking care
of the baby, Tramp,
and her puppies.